I0639504

Frank Beard, Marc Antony Henderson

The Song of Milkanwatha

Frank Beard, Marc Antony Henderson

The Song of Milkanwatha

ISBN/EAN: 9783744767163

Printed in Europe, USA, Canada, Australia, Japan

Cover: Foto ©Andreas Hilbeck / pixelio.de

More available books at **www.hansebooks.com**

THE

SONG OF MILKANWATHA

TRANSLATED FROM

THE ORIGINAL FEEJEE

BY

MARC ANTHONY HENDERSON, D.C.L.

PROFESSOR OF THE FEEJEE LANGUAGE AND LITERATURE IN THE BRANDYWINE
FEMALE ACADEMY

ILLUSTRATED BY FRANK BEARD

" There were who spiritual legends feigned,
Half lofty, half profound, not nigh half true."
PHILIP JAMES BAILEY

THIRD EDITION

ALBANY, N. Y.
D. R. NIVER, 46 N. PEARL STREET
1883

Outing Publishing and Printing Co. [Limited]
Albany, N. Y.

THE SONG OF MILKANWATHA.

" He, of a damsel, with fellow-maidens sporting,
   In vital brilliance dropping through the star-gate
   Of the high luminous land, was born;
   And lifting into life his facial flower,
   Throughout the vast passivity he passed,
   All active; scaling on foot the mount,
   That he his starry ancestry might hail,
   There converse held, with all the eloquent orbs;
   Adown a foamy current, in a skiff,
   Dimpling the wave, he sped; great the show
   Of lawny-weepers, lifted to dim eyes;
   He fainted, asked the watery powers, and at last,
   With eyne by spirit-fire purged, discerned
   How sweet was truth, for death in truth was life,
   Initiate, mystic, perfected, epopt,
   Illuminate, adept, transcendent, he
   Ivy-like lived, and died, and again lived,
   Resuscitant—god of psycho-pompous function.''
                    " THE MYSTIC."—*Philip James Bailey.*

TRANSLATOR'S PREFACE.

A WORD or two with reference to the following POEM, which is now for the first time presented to the civilized world.

That, in many of its parts, there is a strong correspondence between it and Mr. LONGFELLOW'S great work, "The Song of Hiawatha," is too apparent to be overlooked. But so far from basing upon this similarity of incident and treatment, a charge of *literary piracy* against Mr. LONGFELLOW, as has been done by some who have discovered a much fainter likeness to a poem of Scandinavian origin—the translator recognizes in it only another evidence of that unity of thought which characterizes the human species, and which is a natural consequence of the unity of the races, of which the great family of man is composed.

How far the "Song of Hiawatha" may be justly deemed an *imitation*, however, in outline, incident, or versification, of the Scandinavian—or of the poem from the Feejee, here presented to our readers—it is for them, and not for the translator, to decide; but it is believed that a careful comparison, one with another, will disclose many curious resemblances in form and feature, which may be thought worthy the attention of men of letters.

It is hardly necessary to add that, so far as he was able to appreciate the spirit of the Poem, the translator has endeavored faithfully to retain it.

The liberties which he has taken have been verbal only, and such as are unavoidable in transplanting the ideas and emotions of a people from their own language to another.

For example, "Polli-wog-in" has been translated *farmers*, although the use of the word may seem a strange one to those into whose conception of the Feejee character the idea of *industry* has never entered.

The reason, however, is obvious—since our estimates of things are always *relative*, and he who keeps a pig or grows a square yard of potatoes among a people distinctively savage, judged by their standard of labor, is as emphatically a farmer as the man who plows, in America, his hundred acres, and whose cattle graze upon a thousand hills.

Several words and forms of expression which in our language have become obsolete, such as her'n, his'n, ouch, not never, not for no one, did n't nothing, a-rolling, a-sitting, etc., are retained because of their striking analogy to words and expressions representing the same ideas in the Feejee tongue.

The word that designates the Water treatment which we call Hydropathy, is so rendered from the original, "Sit-an'-shiver."

If the objection be made to the scenes and characters as represented in the translation, that they indicate so advanced a stage of social progress as to suggest the probability of their having caught an unconscious coloring from the fancy of the translator, it may be fairly met with the presumption that a closer familiarity with the manners and mode of life of the Feejees, on the part of the reader, would show the invalidity of such objections.

To give an impulse to investigation in this direction is the translator's only motive in publication, and his earnest hope is that this simple Poem may serve to interest the Christian World in the people among whom it is still preserved, and in whose midst he has spent several memorable years.

CLOVER DELL, Feb. 1856.

ARGUMENT.

The Birth and Childhood of the Hero. His Youth. He forms the acquaintance of two singular individuals. Goes courting, and is married. His two friends swept away by the Watta-puddel, or Rushing River, to the land of Ponee-rag-bag, situated farther downward. His wife is seized with chills and fever, and being supposed dead, is thrown into the River, but revived by the sudden shock of the water, is borne in safety to Ponee-rag-bag. The hero, in a fit of temporary insanity, follows her in his skiff. Reaching Ponee-rag-bag, he finds not only his wife, but his friends also, awaiting him. Their strange preservation suggests the Water treatment in disease, and returning with them he becomes the founder of the Hydropathic System.

The scene is laid in the Island of Chaw-a-man-up, one of the Feejee Group.

THE SONG OF MILKANWATHA.

INTRODUCTION.

If an individual person,
Say John Smith,* or John Smith's uncle,
Or some other friend of his'n .
Should propound to me the question,
Whence derived you these traditions
Which you are about to tell us,
With their incidents peculiar ;
These strange legends so mysterious,
With the smell of trees and flowers,
With the sound of brooks and breezes,
With the roaring of the thunder

---

* The name John Smith, which occurs several times in the following introduction, has been employed because, by conventional use, it has come to express
the idea of *man in the concrete.*

Ever sounding, never ceasing,
Going when you think it 's stopping,
Going as a woman's tongue goes,
As a lively woman's tongue goes;

I would speak up, I would tell him,
" From the regions far beyond here,
From the mighty wildernesses
Where the Spoopendykes inhabit,
Where the Noodles pitch their wigwams,
From the hill-tops bare and breezy,
From the valleys soft and mushy,
From the marshes and the duck-ponds,
Where the melancholy bull-frog,
Brek-e-kex-co-ax, the bull-frog,
Sitteth in the slimy waters:

" As I heard them, so I tell them,
Literatim et verbatim,
Just exactly as I heard them

From the mouth of Rumpalumpkin,
Him as played upon the bagpipes,
Played—and sang between the blowings."

And if John Smith, or his uncle,
Or some other friend of his'n,
Should inquire where Rumpalumpkin
Came across these strange traditions;

I would speak up, I would tell him,
" In the trees where climb the squirrels,
In the holes where crouch the woodchucks,
In the cracks the spiders hide in,
In the hornets' nest he found them;

" All—or nearly all—the wildfowl
Sang them, shrieked them, in the marshes,
In the marshes by the duck-ponds;
Pee-nee-wig the turkey-buzzard,
And the gray-goose Dab-si-dido;
Quag the duck, the snipe Lum-bago,
And the long-legged, bush-necked partridge,
Rigdam-bol-le-meta-kimo."

And if John Smith, or his uncle,
Or some other friend of his'n,
Asked me, Who is Rumpalumpkin?
Tell us more of Rumpalumpkin;
I should speak up very quickly,
And reply to him in this way:

" In the valley of Mus-tug-gin,
That extremely verdant valley,
Where, in summer, green the trees were,
Bare and leafless in the winter;
Where the streams flowed in the Summer,
But in Winter time were frozen;
In this very verdant valley,
Lighted by the sparkling waters,
By the forest branches shaded,
Lived the man as played the bagpipes,
Played—and sang between the blowings—
Lived the minstrel Rampalumpkin."

Ye who like this sort of legend,
Like it well enough to listen,
Like the way the thing is done in,

Like a story so unmeaning,
That, to save your life, you cannot
See nor head nor tail un-*to* it,
Tell the end from the beginning—
Listen to this wondrous story,
To this Song of Milkanwatha.

Ye who will not writhe nor wriggle
While I tell this story to you,
Will not look or act uneasy,
But will give your whole attention,
Without gaping, stretching, yawning,
While I tell this story to you;
Listen now, for I will tell it,
Tell it truly, as I told you,
As I told you I would tell it,
On condition, you remember,
That you would not writhe nor wriggle,
But would give your whole attention
Without gaping, stretching, yawning,
While I tell this story to you;
Listen now all ye, I pray you,
Hear this Song of Milkanwatha.

MILKANWATHA'S CHILDHOOD.

Long ago, in days that are not,
In the times that no one knows of,
Right head-foremost thro' the evening
From the shining planet Venus,   .
Swiftly down came Kimo-kairo,
Came the long haired Kimo-kairo,
Married, but without no children.

She was climbing up a plum-tree,
Plum-tree in the planet Venus,
Climbing with some other women,
When, alas, the branch she stood on
Cracked and snapped, because 't was rotten,
Cracked and snapped off quite completely,
And head-foremost thro' the evening,

Fell the long haired Kimo-kairo,
Fell the shrieking Kimo-kairo,
Fell the long-haired, shrieking Kimo,
Down to Plow-e-tup the cornfield,
In the cornfield soft and mushy.
" Look ! a rocket !" said the farmers,
" Some one must have fired a rocket,
'Cause that was the stick that come down."

'Midst the chickweed and the clover,
Lying on some last year's huskings,
In the Plow-e-tup, the cornfield,
Kimo-kairo had a son born,
And she called him Milkanwatha,
Him as is our story's hero,
The real, genuine Milkanwatha.

But alas for Kimo-kairo !
And alas for Milkanwatha !
She, the mother, was so injured
Falling from the planet Venus,
Plum-tree in the planet Venus,

And the Plow-e-tup the cornfield
Was so very cool and open,
Such a breezy place to lie in,
That, to save her life, she could not
Keep from dying while she lay there,
Lay upon the last year's huskings ;
So she died, poor Kimo-kairo,
And beside her, Milkanwatha
Rolled and cried, unhappy baby,
Wond'ring why she did n't nurse him,
Thinking her alive as usual.

There they both were found, next morning,
By the ancient nurse Marcosset ;
Her whom all the neighbors honored
For her skill in nursing sick-folks,
Chiefly, through the chills and fever :
There she found sweet Kimo-kairo
Lying dead upon the huskings ;
And not far off—found our hero,
Very wide awake and kicking.

On the banks of Watta-puddel

Rushing river, Watta-puddel—
Stood the ancient nurse's wigwam,
Stood the wigwam of Marcosset:
Back behind it dark the woods were,
Dark as pitch the woods behind it;
Swift before it rolled the river,
Rolled its torrent ever onward,
Through the long and dismal forests,
Through the mountains and the valleys,
In the sunlight and the moonlight,
Toward the unknown Ponee-rag-bag,
Toward the regions farther downward.

Here Marcosset, ancient female,
Nursed the baby Milkanwatha;
Gave him porridge, gave him catnip,
Gave him pap and water-gruel;
When he fretted, quickly hushed him,

Saying, "Wild-cat, scratch his eyes out."
Saying, "Bulldog, bite his toes off;"
Put him fast asleep by humming,

" Hitta-ka-dink, my duck, my darling,
　Who 's this with the funny snub-nose,'
　Snub-nose, so uncommon snubby?
　Hitta-ka-dink, my duck, my darling."

　　Here he, day by day, grew older,
　Sat alone upon the door-step,
　Heard the summer breezes moaning,
　Heard the waters ever plashing,
　Sounds unusual and peculiar;
" Tizzarizzen," sighed the breezes—
" Splosh-ka-swosh-ky," plashed the river.

　　Here he saw the Melee-wee-git,
　Lightning-bug, the Melee-wee-git,
　Saw the Feesh-go-bang, musquito,
　Saw Snappo, the pinching-beetle,
　Saw the dragon-fly, snap-peter,
　And the flea, too, Sticka-ta-wa-in.

　　Saw above him, in the heavens,
　The Aurora red and glowing—

2

Wondered what it was that did it—
Said, " What is that there, Marcosset? "
And Marcosset up and answered.
" Once an angry boy I know of,
Took and clutched his uncle To-bee,
Took and pitched him, in the evening,
Up into the starry heavens;
Right against the boulder pavement
Of the Milky-way he pitched him,
And his blood and brains went splashing
Over all the sky around there;
That 's what makes them spots upon it—
That is why it 's called Aurora." *

Saw the dazzling planet Venus
Blushing o'er the dark horizon;
Said, " What is that there, Marcosset? "
And Marcosset up and answered,
" That 's the hole your mother fell through,
When she tumbled from the plum-tree—
Plum-tree in the planet Venus—
Down to Plow-e-tup the cornfield."

---

*A capital pun upon this word, in the original, is entirely lost in the trans-
lation.

And whenever, in the evening,
Brek-e-kex-co-ax, the bull-frog,
Made all kinds of dismal noises,
Milkanwatha, trembling, whispered,
" What an awful noise ; what does it ? "
And Marcosset up and answered ;
" 'T is the bull-frog's way of singing,
Singing to another bull-frog
In the marshes and the duck-ponds—
Only that, my Milkanwatha."

So, by slow degrees, it turned out,
That he learned the names of all things,
Of the birds, and beasts, and fishes,
Of the bugs of each description,
How they looked and where they hided,
And their general mode of living ;
So he gained from old Marcosset,
Much important information,
Much which *we* can never know of
In our day and generation—
Our degenerate generation.

II.

MILKANWATHA'S HUNTING.

Now, about this time, Sumpunkin,
He, the jolly wag, Sumpunkin,
He, the crony of Marcosset,
Made a very stylish blow-gun
For our hero, Milkanwatha;
Made it from a stalk of alder,
From a willow made some arrows—
Little arrows for to blow through—
And each arrow had a pin in.

This he gave to Milkanwatha
For to keep, he said, remarking,
" You must go, my little fellow,
Go into the woods behind here,
Go and kill a pretty squirrel,
Go and kill a rather big one.'"

Right into the woods behind there
Ran the gallant Milkanwatha,
With his arrows and his blow-gun :
And he heard the birds exclaiming.
" Do n't you blow at me your arrows,
Blow your arrows with a pin in,
Oh, now, Milkanwatha, do n't you."

Cried the O-pee-pod, the bullfinch,
Cried the Nill-e-pip, the chippy,
· " Do n't you blow at me your arrows,
With a pin in, Milkanwatha."

·

On a stump, not far before him,
Hopped the Lingo-sneedel, smiling,
Hopped the Lingo-sneedel, blue-bird,
Sneezed, and cried out, after sneezing,
" Do n't you blow at me your arrows,
With a pin in, Milkanwatha."

And a little off to one side,
Peeped the Yella-gal, the woodchuck,

Sort o' fear'd and sort o' not so,
Peeped and squeaked to Milkanwatha,
"Do n't you blow at me your arrows,
With a pin in, Milkanwatha."

Onward through the woods behind there
Walked he, stalked he, with his blow-gun,
Heeding not these observations ;
Neither Opee-pod, the bullfinch,
Nor the Nill-e-pip, the chippy,
Nor the Yella-gal, the woodchuck,
Nor the bluebird, Lingo-sneedel—
He was hunting after squirrels,
After squirrels only, *he* was.

Crouching down behind an old log,
Pretty soon he saw a squirrel,
And it was a rather big one ;
Saw a squirrel's head on one side—
Saw a squirrel's tail the other—
Head and tail of one big squirrel :

" He was hunting after squirrels,

Taking in a long breath, very,
Milkanwatha aimed his blow-gun—
Blew through with the long breath, very,
With the long breath that he took in;
Squirrel's tail a moment quivered,
Squirrel closed his eyes a moment,
Turned a somerset, completely,
And lay dead upon the old log;
For the arrow with the pin in,
To his brain had penetrated,
Like a big musquito stung him.

In the wilderness, behind there,
Far behind Marcosset's wigwam,
Far away from Watta-Puddel,
Lay defunct Peek-week, the squirrel—
Lay without a breath or motion,
Hearing not the breezes' sighing,
Hearing not their Tizzarizzen,
As they moaned his sad condition,
As they sobbed, amid the branches,
O'er the death that he had come to,
O'er his speedy dissolution.

But the victor, in his triumph,
Jumped and waved his hat, exulting
O'er the death that he had come to,
O'er his speedy dissolution :
And, with eager haste, he ran home,
In one hand Peek-week, the squirrel,
In the other hand the blow-gun—
Fearful instrument, the blow-gun ;
And Marcosset and Sumpunkin,
Kissed him, 'cause he killed the squirrel,
'Cause it was a rather big one.

From the s
Made some m
Mittens with
With the fur-s
So 's to keep
That was why
Why she put

From the other parts Marcosset,
From the lungs, and lights, and liver,

Brain, and heart, and spinal marrow—
Made a squirrel chowder for him;
And their friends dropped in to eat some;
Smacked their lips, while they were eating,
'Cause 't was such a tender squirrel;
Smacked the lips of Milkanwatha,
After they had finished eating,
'Cause he was so bold a hunter,
Called him Good-boy, Mulee-donkee,
Called him Bráve-boy, Spoo-ne-boo-be.

III.

MILKANWATHA'S YOUTH AND EARLY MANHOOD.

MILKANWATHA, now, was older—
Older, bigger than he had been
Since his mother, Kimo-kairo,
In the cornfield came and bore him.
None were half as big as he was,
None were half as tall as he was,
None were half as strong as he was;
None could lift the things that he could,
None could catch the things that he could,
None could eat the things that he could;
No one ever laughed so loudly,
As he laughed, when something funny
Happened for to come across him;
Ever saw such sights as he did,
Ever thrashed so many rascals,
Ever kissed so many damsels,
Ever nursed so many children.

He could take and fire an arrow—
Run right after—go right by it—
Then stop short and say, distinctly,
Always "Jac," and sometimes, "Robbin-sun,"
Ere the lazy arrow got there.

He could take and throw a stone so,
Throw it right up over-head so,
At the moment when the sun set,
That it would n't think of dropping,
Till the sun came up, next morning,
Till the Doodel-doo, the rooster,
Crowed the daylight up next morning.

He could do the Cutta-dido—
Cut the pigeon's wing, so quickly,
That his heels would strike together,
Eighty times and even ninety—
Once he did it ninety-nine times—
One more would have made the hundred.

He had leggins, Roota-ba-ga,
That were quite peculiar leggins ;

When they were put on and buttoned,
He could step from here to yonder,
Step from here, 'way over yonder,
Step right up on the horizon,
And converse there, with the full moon.

He had Clog-a-logs, moreover,
Boots—with which on one occasion,
While conversing with the full moon,
On the edge of the horizon,
He, so fiercely, kicked his foot out,
That he hit the constellation,
Thimbel-nubbin, or Big Dipper,
Kicked a hole right in the bottom,
So that all the water ran through,
Which was put there, for the Great Bear,
For to come and wash his feet in. ·

All the eagles of the mountains
Flew far over Milkanwatha ;
All the wild beasts of the forest
Trembled, when he strided toward them,
Fled into the shadows trembling.

All the old men praised his courage,
All the young men owned him strongest,   .
All the women wished for children,
Wished for sons as brave as he was;
All the maidens gazed upon him,
Gazed with silent admiration,
Gazed with beating hearts and blushes,
As he passed their lonely wigwams,
And returned with sighs and weeping,
To their usual avocations;
Wishing, as they darned their stockings—
Scrubbed, and baked, and swept, and dusted,
Did clear-starching, did crochet-ing,
Made pincushions, always heart-shaped,
Fastened, two and two together,
Pierced all o'er with pins like arrows,
Arrows from an unseen archer—
Wishing that a gallant lover,
That a lover, like our hero,
Soon might come, and sit beside them
In their wigwams; each one wishing
He was her'n, and she was his'n,
Ever her'n, and ever his'n,
Her'n and his'n, now and ever;

Each one wishing for our hero—
But he wishing not for no one ;
Having other things to think of,
Other fish upon his griddle,
Other fish to fry upon it.

"Silli-nimkum, the sweet piper,
And the very fat man, Bee-del."

He had been, for six months, rolling,
Six month: and a little over;
Rolling on from morn to evening,
And from season unto season,
Through all countries, nations, climates,
Past the zones and past the tropics,
Past the line of the equator,
Ever onward, forward, downward,
Till he got to where he came from—
Till he all the earth had rolled round.

These two persons, just referred to,
Silli-ninkum, the sweet piper,
And the very fat man, Bee-del,
As I 've mentioned, were the couple—
Were the friends of Milkanwatha—
Whom he liked uncommon strongly;
And these three, this faithful trio,
Never quarrelled with each other,
Never gossipped, never back-bit,
Never acted mean, as some do,
But they did as they 'd be done by,
And they often met together,

And indulged in conversation
In a free and easy manner.

V.

MILKANWATHA'S COURTSHIP AND MARRIAGE.

JUST as, to a big umbrella,
Is the handle, when it's raining,
So a wife is, to her husband;
Though the handle do support it,
'T is the top keeps all the rain off;
Though the top gets all the wetting,
'T is the handle bears the burden;
So the top is good for nothing,
If there is n't any handle,
And the case holds, vice versa.

In this way, did Milkanwatha
Reason, when he was a-thinking,
Thinking of his Pogee-wogee,
Of the blue-eyed Sweet Potato,
In the village of the Noodles.

"Marry some one, living round here,"
Said the ancient nurse, Marcosset;
"Do n't go looking over yonder,
For to find a wife to marry:
As a stick of maple candy,
Is the homeliest girl around here;
As a lozenge or a gum-drop
Is the prettiest over yonder."

And thus answered Milkanwatha;
"Very true, dear old Marcosset,
Mighty sweet is maple candy,
But I much prefer a lozenge—
Very much prefer a gum-drop."

Said Marcosset, "Do n't you go, now,
For to get a girl to marry,
Knowing nothing whatsoever;
Bring one as can do clear-starching,
Sew, and knit, and run of errands,
And be generally useful—
That 's the sort of girl to marry."

Milkanwatha answered, cheerful:
"In the regions far beyond here,
Where the Noodles pitch their wigwams,
Pogee-wogee, Sweet-Potato,
Charming female is residing;
I will go and fetch her to you,
And she 'll make herself convenient,
Sew, and knit, and do clear-starching,
Be your lozenge, be your gum-drop,
Be your stick of maple candy."

"Do n't you go now," said Marcosset,
"Go and fetch an unknown female,
Do n't you go and fetch a Noodle—
Awful strange folks, are the Noodles."

Then replied our Milkanwatha;
"That 's exactly why I do it,
'Cause they 're strange, and must n't be so;
We must make ourselves acquainted,
We must go and call upon them."
Saying which, our hero, boldly,

Travelled to the regions northward,
Past the dreary wildernesses,
Where the Spoopendykes inhabit,
To the village of the Noodles.

He had put on Roota-ba-ga,
Buttoned on the magic leggins,
And, although he kept a-stepping,
From one hill-top to another,
Over cornfields, soft and mushy,
Over marshes, goose-ponds, duck-ponds,
Yet he seemed a long while, getting
To the home of Pogee-wogee,
To the village of the Noodles.

Shortly previous to arriving,
He perceived a woodchuck, peeping—
Peeping from his hole, for fresh air,
'Cause 't was badly ventilated,
But the woodchuck didn't see him;
So he took and kicked his foot out,
And he knocked the woodchuck's .brains out—

Just as when he hit the bottom
Of the Dipper, Thimbel-nubbin,⁴
All the water went and ran through,
Which was put there, for the Great Bear,
For to come and wash his feet in.

Then he took the woodchuck with him,
For a gift to Pogee-wogee;
"Who is that?" inquired a Noodle—
"That's the hero Milkanwatha;"
"What's he got?" "He's got a woodchuck."

Pogee-wogee's loving grandma
At the front door sat, a-knitting,
And, beside her, Sweet-Potato,
Charming female, was a-sitting.
Looking somewhat melancholy.

The old lady's mind was busy-
Busy as her trembling fingers;

Far away her thoughts were flitting,
Midst the days so long departed,
Midst the memories of girlhood,
Midst the sunny moments flitting;
Flitting midst them, as, so often,
She had seen, in youthful rambles
With the dear ones gone forever,
Bees, on restless wing pass lightly,
Lightly on from flower to flower,
Humming low, melodious music,
Sporting, gayly, in the sunshine.

Pogee's thoughts were busy also,
Busy as her grandma's fingers;
She was thinking of our hero,
Wond'ring why she 'd never met him,
Never heard his well-known footstep,
Never seen his sturdy figure,
Since that time when they had parted,
Since that sunny summer morning.

In the midst of these reflections,
Midst the thoughts, that passed before them,

Unexpected, round a corner,
Rather wet with perspiration,
Holding in his hand the woodchuck,
Came the lover—ardent lover
Of the Noodle, Pogee-wogee,
Came the son of Kimo-kairo,
Came the joyous Milkanwatha.

Ancient grandame stopped her knitting,
Laid the stocking in the window,
Asked him to come in, remarking,
"Glad to see you, Milkanwatha."

In the lap of Pogee-wogee
Milkanwatha laid the woodchuck,
And she looked at him so tender,
That his blood ran cold within him,
Saying, with a bashful softness,
"Very happy for to see you—
Very much so, Milkanwatha."

Soon as he was seated, almost,

Pogee-wogee fetched refreshments,
'Cause he looked so hot and tired,
'Cause he had such perspiration;
Fetched him in some "floating island,"
Interspersed with pickled walnuts,
Which he much preferred of all things; ·
And a little mug of cider,
For to take and wash it down with,
Wash the floating isle and walnuts,
Isle and pickled walnuts down with.

Not a word spoke Pogee-wogee,
But she heard the conversation
Going on, while he was feeding,
Heard him tell of old Marcosset—
How she found him, how she nursed him,
Gave him porridge, gave him catnip,
Gave him pap and water gruel;
Heard him tell of Silli-ninkum,
And the very fat man, Bee-del—
How the former piped uncommon,
And the latter rolled the earth round;
Heard him give a fine description

Of the scenery about there,
On the banks of Watta-puddel.

"You have never been to see us,
On the banks of Watta-puddel—
You nor any other Noodles;
Shall we never scrape acquaintance?"
Said the ardent Milkanwatha.
"That this may 'be obviated,
State of things be put a stop to,
S'pose you give me Pogee-wogee,
For to be a wife un-*to* me—
Sweet-Potato, charming female,
Much the handsomest of Noodles."

For some minutes, the old lady
Smoked her solemn pipe in silence;
Putting on her glasses, slowly,
First she looked at Pogee-wogee,
Then she looked at Milkanwatha;
"It depends on Pogee-wogee—
What's your feeling on the subject?
Speak your mind and heart out, Pogee."

And the charming Sweet-Potato,
To the very ear-tips blushing,
With a dubious expression,
Crossed the wigwam to her lover,
Drew her stool up, saying faintly,
"You may have me, if you want to—
I 'll go with you, Milkanwatha."

Such was Milkanwatha's courting,
This was just the way he did it,
Bore his darling, Pogee-wogee,
From her grandma's lonely cabin,
From the village of the Noodles;
Back he bore her thro' the forests,
Over hills, and over valleys,
To the ancient nurse's wigwam—
To the wigwam of Marcosset.

All along the line of travel,
Birds were singing to the lovers,
Songs of welcome 'mid the branches,
Songs of warm congratulation,

And the bugs joined in the chorus;
Sang the Opee-pod, the bullfinch,
Sang the Nille-pip, the chippy,
Sang the bluebird, Lingo-Sneedel;
Hummed the Feesh-go-bang, musquito,
Hummed Snappo, the pinching-beetle,
And the dragon-fly, Snap-peter;
"Ain't it lucky, ain't it lucky,
Jolly luck for Pogee-wogee,
Jolly luck for Milkanwatha."

So he fetched her to Marcosset,
Fetched the lozenge, fetched the gum-drop,
Fetched the stick of maple candy,
Pogee-wogee, Sweet-Potato,
Best beloved of female Noodles.

They arrived on Tuesday morning,
And were married Thursday evening;
All day Tuesday, old Marcosset,
Made her pies and preparations;
All day Wednesday, boys were running

Up and down, throughout the village,
For to leave a soda-cracker,
At the door of every wigwam,
As a card of invitation—
As a sign that Milkanwatha
Meditated matrimony.

Thursday came, and Thursday evening,
And the neighbors, also, with it;
Fast they crowded in the wigwam,
Crowded in the pies and puddings,
Which Marcosset made, on Tuesday;
But the bride, nor bridegroom neither,
Didn't eat a bit of nothing,
Only waited on the others,
Only watched the pies and puddings
Disappearing, in succession,
In the stomachs of the people.

When the eating part was over,
There was singing, piping, dancing,
And the evening went so swiftly,
That it left the guests behind it,
Left them, 'mid the hours of morning.

Then they called for Silli-ninkum,
For to sing a song at parting,
And he came, the skillful piper,
Him as always was obliging,
Piping, when requested for to;
Came, and sang the song that follows,
Sang the verses, 'twixt the blowings,
Sang a female's lamentation,
For her lover, her Bee-no-nee.

"When I think of him I love so,
Oh dear! think of him I love so,
When I am a-thinking of him—
    Ouch! my sweetheart, my Bee-no-nee.

"Oh dear! when we left each other,
He presented me a thimble,
As a pledge, a silver thimble—
    Ouch! my sweetheart, my Bee-no-nee!

"'I'll go 'long with you,' he whispered,
'Oh my! to the place you came from,

4

Let me go along,' he whispered—
　　Ouch! my sweetheart, my Bee-no-nee!

"'It 's awful fur, full fur,' I answered,
'Fur away it is,' I answered,
'Oh my, yes! the place I come from'—
　　Ouch! my sweetheart, my Bee-no-nee!

"As I looked round for to see him,
Where I left him, for to see him,
He was looking for to see me—
　　Ouch! my sweetheart, my Bee-no-nee!

"On the log he was a-sitting,
On the hollow log a-sitting,
That was chopped down by somebody!—
　　Ouch! my sweetheart, my Bee-no-nee!

"When I think of him I love so,
Oh my! think of him I love so,
When I am a-thinking of him—
　　Ouch! my sweetheart, my Bee-no-nee!"

When this mournful song was ended,
All the folks seemed in a hurry
For to go, and so they did it,
Leaving there the nurse Marcosset,
With the bride and with the bridegroom;
And they all three started eating,
And continued so till morning—
Till the Doodel-doo, the rooster,
Crowed the daylight up next morning.

VI.

PA-PA-MAMA.

You shall hear how Pa-pa-mama,
Pogee-wogee's whilome lover,
In the village of the Noodles,
Came one time to Watta-puddel ;
How he showed himself a coward,
How he proved himself a rascal,
How he reached his dissolution.

It was in the sprinkly Spring-time,
That he came to Watta-puddel,
Came with bitter thoughts inside him.
Came to be revenged on Pogee,
'Cause she had in times departed,
When he asked her to be his'n,
Strongly urged her to be his'n—

Said with pitying glance, but firmly,
" Never your'n, O Pa-pa-mama !
No," she muttered, " never his'n."

Through the village sneaking came he,
At the dusky hour of twilight,
When the people all were gathered
As their custom was to do so,
Met together, story-telling,
In the fat man Bee-del's wigwam ;
Just as Bee-del was describing
What he witnessed while a-rumbling,
All the earth around a-rumbling
On his swift, mysterious journey.
And the people listened to him,
Winking when he was n't looking,
Much as if to say " We know him,
Know him we do, you and me do."

He had seen, he said, a river
Bigger than the Watta-puddel,
And so muddy too, said Bee-del,

That a spoon stands straight up in it!
And the people pointed slowly
Over the left shoulder, saying,
"Oh now, Bee-del, what a story,
Boo," they said, " you 're telling, Bee-del."

On this river deep and muddy,
Swam a monster like a sturgeon,
Fatter than ten thousand sturgeons,
And his fins, instead of flapping,
Round and round continued turning,
Quite as fast as I myself did.
" Boo ! " the people cried together,
" Boo ! " they said, " it 's such a big one."

On his head, he said, were growing,
Straight and tall as is the pine tree,
Two black tusks all hollow inside;
And his breath, so dark and dismal,
Dark as thunder-clouds in summer,
Through them rolled forth o'er the river,
Darkening all the landscape over.
" Boo ! " they said, " it 's Bee-del talking."

Round his mouth, like summer lightning,
Flames of fire flashed in the darkness,
And the monster, while a-swimming,
Shrieked so wildly that the echoes
On the far-off misty hill-sides,
On the hill-sides far below there,
Up and answered to his shrieking,
Answered as the tigress answers
To the tiger in the forest.
" Boo ! " they said, "a likely story !"

On his back were huddled, shrinking,
Men and women, pale and shrinking,
Pale-faced as the moon in winter ;
Borne off by the fiery monster—
For the prey of him and his'n,
Borne off, as the tiger swiftly
Bears his victim through the darkness,
Bears it to his forest hiding.
And the people winking, whispered,
" What a liar is our Bee-del !
Boo ! " they said, " what lies he tells us."

"Turned the table bottom upside,
Turned the chairs all upside downside."

In the meantime, Pa-pa-mama
Stealing through the silent evening
Reached the wigwam of Marcosset;
" No one here," he said, rejoicing.
" Coast all clear," he said, exulting ;
" All the folks have gone to Bee-del's."

With a mushy step he entered,
Turned the tables bottom upside,
Turned the chairs all upside downside,
Kicked the boiling kettle over,
Piled the bed clothes in the corner,
Crammed the bolster up the chimney,
For to trouble Pogee-wogee,
For to make Marcosset angry ;
After which he started homeward
On his stealthy journey started.

When our hero, shortly after,
Came and saw the wild disorder,
" Not so long," said he, " his legs are,
But I 'll catch this fellow quickly."

'Bout a mile or so he 'd travelled,
On the track of Pa-pa-mama,

When he saw, just on before him,
Pa-pa-mama disappearing,
Slowly sinking in a mud-hole,
Saw his head just going under;
And he stepped up very briskly,
Shouting down into the mud-hole,
"Never more, O Pa-pa-mama!
Will you drop into our wigwam;
You have dropped in once too often.
Turned the tables are forever,
You have done your final dropping;"
Then the hole closed up forever.

But the people of the village
Still remember Pa-pa-mama;
And whenever in the winter,
While they're sitting story telling,
Comes the storm wind from the Northland,
Rattling all the doors and windows, .
Drifting snow around the wigwams;
"Lo," they say, "'t is Pa-pa-mama.
Turning all things wrong side upside,
Turning all things upside downside—
'T is that Pa-pa-mama's doings."

VII.

THE FEVER AND THE AGUE.

FIFTEEN summers, fifteen winters,
Fifteen springs and fourteen autumns,
Full of joys and full of sorrows,
Now had passed since Milkanwatha
Bore the beauteous Pogee-wogee
To the banks of Watta-Puddel;
Full of joys, with wife and children,
Full of griefs, for friends departed.

Silli-ninkum, the sweet piper,
Him as piped as no one else piped,
He had passed to Ponee-rag-bag,
To the regions down the river;
He had done his final piping
On the banks of Watta-Puddel.

Going out, one winter morning,
For a little private skating,
Lo! the ice gave way beneath him!
Lo! the chilling waters siezed him,
Bore him, struggling, ever downward,
To the country far below there,
To the regions down the river!

Bee-del, too, was there no longer,
Milkanwatha's friend, the fat man;
He had left the field of action,
Left the banks of Watta-puddel.

Since the piper had departed
He had grown a great deal fatter,
In his grief for having lost him,
Grown so fat he seldom waddled
Through the village as aforetime,
Only hung around the wigwam,
Sprawled himself out in the sunshine.

But one day, in fiery August,
After quite a hearty dinner,

He went down, he rolled himself down,
To the river for to bathe there,
As in days so long departed,
When he washed himself more often;
Far into the stream he waded,
And, alas! the current seized him!
As it seized poor Silli-ninkum;
In its wild embrace it clasped him,
And by reason of his fatness—
Of his stomach's monstrous fatness,
Which prevented him from striking,
Striking out his legs as usual—
He was carried, like a bladder,
Floating on the turbid waters,
To the land of Ponee-rag-bag,
To the regions farther downward.

Never jumps a sheep that's frightened,
Over any fence whatever,
Over wall, or fence, or timber,
But a second follows after,
And a third, upon the second,
And a fourth, and fifth, and so on,

First a sheep, and then a dozen,
Till they all, in quick succession,
One by one have got clean over:

So misfortunes, almost always,
Follow after one another,
Seem to watch each other, always ·
When they see the tail uplifted,
In the air the tail uplifted,
As the sorrow leapeth over;
Lo ! they follow, thicker, faster,
Till the air of earth seems darkened,
With the tails of sad misfortunes,
Till our hearts, within us, weary,
Cry out: "Are there more a-coming?"

So, alas, our Milkanwatha,
Ten years after he was married,
In that most uncommon winter,
Cried out: "Are there more a-coming?"

Oh, that most uncommon winter !
Oh, that sneezy freezy winter !

Ever faster! faster!! faster!!!
Fell the snow, on vale and hill-side;
Ever colder! colder!! colder!!!
Swept the wild winds from the Northland,
Swept the storm-wind Gus-ta-blo-za!
It was really inconvenient,
Merely to step out a moment,
And to go to any distance,
'Less you muffled up, completely,
In your tippet´ and your mittens,
Was n't possible, by no means,
Without getting badly frost-bit.

Oh! the Fever and the Ague!
Oh! the burning of the Fever!
Oh! the shaking of the Ague!
Oh! the way the children took it!
Oh! the way the mothers, also,
Took the Fever and the Ague!!

To the ancient nurse's wigwam,
Came the two unpleasant strangers,

Came, without an invitation,
Sat them down by Pogee, boldly,
Staring at the female Noodle !
One of them spoke up, remarking,
"I am Fever, Doan-chu-no-me !"
And the other one continued,
"I am Ague, Wot-el-sha-ku ! !"

But the frightened Pogee, shrinking,
Kept a-shaking and a-burning,
'Cause the Fever and the Ague,
Came and sat so close beside her,
'Cause they stared so steady at her.

Right into the woods behind there,
Swiftly, madly, Milkanwatha
Rushed to go and fetch the doctors—
All the doctors round about there ;
And the ancient nurse Marcosset,
She so skilled in chills and fever,
Gave her warm drinks for to cure her,
For to try and take the chill off.

Then the doctors, Nau-she-atus,
Six in all, came in to see her;
Two and two, they came together,
Came and marched, three times, around her;

Then went up *one* to the bed-side,
"Put your tongue out, Pogee-wogee."
Hi-ai-ai! said all the doctors,
Ho-ang-ho! the queer old doctors,
And another went, observing,
Pogee-wogee 's got the Ague;
Hi-ai-ai! said all the doctors,
Ho-ang-ho! the queer old doctors.
And a third one followed, saying,
Pretty soon she 'll have the Fever;
Hi-ai-ai! said all the doctors—
Ho-ang-ho! the queer old doctors.
Then the other three did likewise;
After which, they marched together,
Two and two, around the bedstead,
Marched out from Marcosset's wigwam,
In the manner they had entered;
Hi-ai-ai! the wise old doctors—
Ho-ang-ho! the wondrous doctors.

5

But, alas, for Pogee-wogee!
And, alas, for Milkanwatha!
She, the loveliest of Noodles,
Was so scorched up by the Fever,
So much shook up by the Ague,
That she spoke nor moved no longer,
And our hero, disappointed,
Wrapt her in a heavy blanket,
In the very neatest manner,
'Cording to the village custom;
And they bore her to the river,
In a long and sad procession;
And they stood and dropped her in it,
As their custom was to do so;
And the eager waters clasped her,
Bore her body, as it had done,
In the case of him, the piper,
In the case of him the fat man,
To the land of Ponee-rag-bag,
To the regions farther downward.

"Float on down," said Milkanwatha,
"Float on down, my duck, my darling,

Very soon, I 'll follow after,
To the regions down the river,
I shall be along, my darling,
Be along, my duck, directly,
Be along, my duck, my darling—
Float on, float, and keep a-floating."

VIII.

MILKANWATHA'S DEPARTURE TO PONEE-RAG-BAG.

GOING now among the people,
On the banks there, standing, gazing,
"Lo!" he told them, "I am going,
I am going, now, to leave you,
Going down the Watta-puddel,
To the region of the sunset,
To the hole the sun drops into,
Over yonder red horizon—
Where you 've often seen me standing,
And conversing with the full-moon—
And I shan't be back, at present,
Not for quite a lengthy season;
Take care of yourselves, my people,
Take much care," said Milkanwatha.

Then he quickly pushed his skiff off,
Got aboard and floated in it,

Down the river's rushing current,
In the sunlight, and the moonlight,
Floating towards the Western sunset—
On his silent journey floated ;
And the people standing, gazing,
Saw him bobbing, bobbing, bobbing,
Up and down upon the river,
Saw his Lawni-weeper waving,
Saw his handkerchief a-waving,
Far adown the Watta-puddel ;
And they all continued calling,
"Good-bye, good-bye, Milkanwatha ;"
And the gray goose, Dab-si-di-do,
O'er the troubled waters flying,
Screamed out, "Good-bye, Milkanwatha ;"
And the Yalla-gal, the woodchuck,
Squeaked out, "Good-bye, Milkanwatha ;"
And the melancholy bull-frog,
Brek-e-kex-co-ax, the bull-frog,
On the river's slimy margin,
Echoed, "Good-bye, Milkanwatha."

So it was that Milkanwatha,
Him as is our story's hero,

Floated down the Rushing river,
Floated thro' the fields and forests,
Thro' the vales and mountains floated,
Ever bobbing, bobbing, bobbing,
In the moonlight and the sunlight,
To the country of the sunset,
To the regions farther downward,
To the land of Ponee-rag-bag,
Far adown the Rushing river—
Rushing river, Watta-puddel.

CONCLUSION.

WHEN the hero of our legend
Reached the land of Ponee-rag-bag,
Reached the hole the sun drops into,
Lo ! an unexpected pleasure
Waited for him, on the landing;
In her blanket wet and dripping,
Just as much alive as usual,
Stood there, smiling, on the landing,
Pogee—loveliest of Noodles.

For the water's sudden coldness,
From her silent stupor waked her,
From the swooning of the Fever,
Which, in vain, the wise old doctors,
Which the Ague, vainly shaking,
Tried to make her wake up out of,
In the wigwam of Marcosset;

And our hero, rushing to her,
Clasped her in his arms, exclaiming,

" Lo ! I see my duck, my darling,
    See the moral of this matter,
    See the lesson that it teaches;
    What the Allopathic Practice
    Was unable to accomplish,
    Lo ! how quickly was effected
    By the Plunge-bath, and the Blanket,
    By the use of *Hydropathy :*
    We must go back, Pogee darling,
    Oh dear ! to the place we come from,
    We must hasten to our people,
    And disclose to them this system,
    Glorious system—Hydropathy."

    And they found there Silli-ninkum,
    And the fat man, Bee-del, also,
    In the same mysterious manner
    Rescued from the hand of Danger—
    From the jaws of Dissolution ;
    And they all went back together,
    And he told the grateful people
    How to drive off all diseases,

By the Plunge-bath and the Blanket—
By the use of Hydropathy.

To this day, they are residing,
Free from fear of chills and fever—
"Worst of ills that flesh is heir to,"
Darkest shadow o'er our pathway,
From the present to the future,
From the 'is now' to the 'shall be'—
To this hour they are residing
In their village, by the river;
And our hero *doubly* liveth—
On the banks of Watta-puddel—
In the hearts of all his people,
Whom he taught the Bath and Blanket—
Glorious System—Hydropathy.

NOTES.

PAGE 13. *Brek-e-kex-co-ax, the bull frog.*

The scholar will be reminded of the " Frogs " of Aristo-
phanes. The word is one of a vast number which might be
referred to, in evidence of the fact, that " Feejee," and
"Greek," are derived from a common root—and the translator
has no hesitation in asserting his conviction, that the early
inhabitants of Greece—the Pelasgians—were colonists from these
islands. The question is much too large for discussion here.

PAGE 2. *Literatim et verbatim.*

The introduction of this familiar Latinism will not, it is
hoped, be deemed in bad taste, when it is remembered that
our own language furnishes no proper substitute. In the
original it reads, " Li-ka-zak-lee, Jus-sa-zak-lee."

PAGE 7. *Kimo-kairo, or Pretty Pollie.*

It is a favorite name with the Feejese. It is probably taken
from the fable of the " Parrot and the Partridge," a verse of which

is quoted below—dropping, of course, the Feejee characters, but retaining, as nearly as possible, the sound of the original:

> " Kimo-kairo, delto mairo,
> Kimo-kairo kimo?
> Strim-stram pom a diddel,
> Lath-a-bon-ne, rig-dam—
> Rig-dam-bol-le-meta-kimo."

PAGE 21. *Always " Jac," and sometimes " Robbin-sun."*

The reader will perceive, that to this language we are indebted for the expression; "Before you can say Jack Robinson."

PAGE 23. *Did clear-starching, did crochet-ing.*

It is believed that these terms more nearly define to the English mind the nature of the operations alluded to, than any others. Goats' milk, however, is used instead of starch— and its effect is to soften, rather than to stiffen the material. All work of the latter sort—knitting, netting, etc., is done upon the thumbs, without the aid of needles, in a manner which cannot be described.

PAGE 31. *Just as to a big umbrella.*

Umbrellas are known to have been in common use in these islands, from the earliest times. They are, invariably, constructed of sheet tin.

PAGE 39. *Putting on her glasses, slowly.*

The Feejee women, of all ages, are proverbially near-sighted.

In the other islands of the Pacific, the phrase, "as blind as a Feejee," is often heard. The date of the invention of spectacles is unknown.

PAGE 40. *To the very ear-tips blushing.*

This expression is remarkable—not because of its poetic merit only—but from the fact that it has been adopted by two poets of our own. In Keats' Endymion, we find, "those ears,

> "Whose tips are glowing hot."

and in the "Life Dráma," by the "modern Shakspeare," as Alexander Smith has been aptly designated by several of the prominent English reviews, occurs the line

> "Hot to the ear-tips, with great thumps of heart."

PAGE 67. *Worst of ills that flesh is heir to.*

The striking parallelism between this line,' and the oft quoted passage from Hamlet's Soliloquy:

> "The thousand natural shocks that flesh is heir to,"

may excite some surprise. In the poem, it will be seen that it appears as a quotation—not from the English bard, as some might suppose—but from Tremen-jus, a Feejee poet who flourished about the year 13. We give the passage in which it occurs, put into the mouth of a war-chief, while vainly endeavoring to devour an old enemy, captured in battle.

> "Thou tough soul! eating of whom be toil!
> Juiceless, thin, of bone compact, and sinew,

> Whereto pertain'th flavor, deathful strong;
> Not for food adapt, save of swiny herd,
> Boar-marshalled, tiger thunder-begotten,
> Or solar wolf! Famished were I,
> Youthfuller, such as not, then less heeded;
> Thus being, cannot I meat introduct
> Of mould o'er-tasteful, all pervasive, rank,
> Of ills flesh be th' heir to, worst much, may be!"

It must be borne in mind, however, that the poem in question was written in ruder times.

At the period of the translator's residence in Chaw-a-man-up, the practice of cannibalism had been, for many years, abandoned, and in other islands of the group, the minds of the people were so far enlightened, that human flesh was indulged in only on Sundays.

PAGE 67. *Whom he taught the Bath and Blanket.*

The period of the introduction of the Water treatment into this island cannot be definitely fixed, but it is supposed to vary little from the date of the Downfall of the Roman Empire.

Milkanwatha, the hero of the Legend and the founder of the System, now ranks among the highest of the Feejee divinities. His name is held religiously sacred, and he is always addressed, as the "god of the psycho-pompous function."

Much additional information concerning him, may be found in the translator's forthcoming work, "The Cyclopædia of Feejee Literature."

VOCABULARY.

Brek-e-kex-co-ax	*Bull-frog*
Bee-del	*Fat Man*
Bee-no-nee	*Dear darling*
Boo	*Pshaw*
Clog-a-logs	*Boots*
Cutta-dido	*Pigeon's wing*
Doan-chu-no-me	*Fever*
Doo-del-doo	*Rooster*
Feesh-go-bang	*Musquito*
Gusta-blo-za	*Storm-wind*
Hi-ai-ai	*Yes, of course*
Hitta-ka-dink	*Lullaby*
Ho-ang-ho	*Yes, by all means*
Kimo-kairo	*Pretty Pollie*
Lawni-weeper	*Handkerchief*
Lingo-sneedel	*Bluebird*
Lum-ba-go	*Snipe*
Mar-cos-set	*Ancient nurse*
Me-le-wee-git	*Lightning-bug*
Milkanwatha	*Star-born*
Mulee-donkee	*Good boy*
Mus-tug-gin	*Verdant valley*

73

Spoopendykes .	*Feejee tribe*
Nil-le-pip	*Chippie*
Noodles .	*Feejee tribe*
Nau-she-a-tus	*Doctors*
O-pee-pod	*Bullfinch*
Pa-pa-mama	*Storm-fool*
Peek-week	. *Squirrel*
Pee-ne-wig	*Turkey-buzzard*
Plow-e-tup	*Corn-field*
Po-gee-wo-gee	- *Sweet-potato*
Po-nee-rag-bag	*Land-far-down*
Quag . . .	*Duck*
Rig-dam-bol-le-met-a-kimo	*Partridge*
Roo-ta-ba-ga .	. *Magic leggins*
Rum-pa-lum-kin	*Sweet singer*
Snap-po	*Pinching-beetle*
Snap-peter .	, *Dragon-fly*
Silli-ninkum .	. *Sweet piper*
Splosh-ka-swosh-ky	*Sound of water*
Sticka-ta-wa-in	. *Flea*
Spoo-ne-boo-be	*Brave boy*
Sum-punk-in	*Jolly wag*
Wot-el-sha-ku	*Ague*
Thimbel-nubbin	*Big Dipper*
Tiz-za-riz-zen	*Sound of breezes*
Watta-puddel	*Rushing river*
Yal-la-gal	*Woodchuck*

ADDITIONAL POEMS.

TO

LAFFAN GROFATTE,

SWISS CONSUL AT CHAWAMANUP,

WHOM I REGARD AS A HUMAN BEING AND
RESPECT AS AN INDIVIDUAL,

THESE MINOR POEMS,

TRANSLATED AT HIS SUGGESTION,

ARE AFFECTIONATELY DEDICATED.

M. A. H.

PREFATORY TO SMALLER POEMS.

THE POEMS which follow are added, not by reason of their supposed superiority to· other works of a similar character within the range of Feejee literature, but because, like the "Song of Milkanwatha," they so nearly resemble familiar productions by distinguished authors.

This resemblance the reader can hardly fail to recognize, since in some minds it has laid the foundation of a belief that many poems, hitherto regarded as the legitimate progeny of the English muse, are, after all, nothing more than parodies upon Feejee originals: a theory which we might less emphatically reject,—did not the reputation of the authors in question forbid us to harbor, for one moment, the suspicion that they could descend from their high position as men and poets—to attack a struggling literature like the Feejee, with a weapon so unworthy of their powers as the Parody—so universally condemned by the rules of the literary "service."

Beyond the desire, therefore, of pointing out these new curiosities of literature, the translator has no wish to say aught that might subject the writings of either language to unfair comparison with those of the other. He is too jealous

of the interests of English literature, to institute an inquiry
which might depreciate the merits of the gifted few whom the
world has ever delighted to honor, and he should go down
to a speedy and uneasy grave, were he conscious of having
torn a sprig from the laurel wreath that binds the brow of
a single one of the sweet singers of England or America.

That they may see for themselves, however, the likeness
referred to, the translator lays before his readers the Feejee
ballads, and side by side with them the opening lines of their
English *parallelographs*, (if the use of such a word may be
allowed,) believing that, awakened by such familiar tones, the
remaining verses will flutter lightly forth from their nesting-
place in the memory and heart.

THE CREEK

(AN IDYDL.)

" Here by this brook, we parted: I to the East,
And he for Italy—too late—too late."
"THE BROOK."—*Alf. Tennyson.*

HERE, by this log, we shook Good-bye ; for good ;
I starting home, and he for Borneo,
With one lung left, and that one tubercled ;
Poor boy—poor boy ; fonder of making rhymes
Than money he, and loving verses bet-
Ter far than better things ; he ne'er could see
How money grew ; it sprouted not, he knew,
Nor had it seed ; how strange, he often said ;
Yet he himself made verses out of naught
But air. Oh, would he 'd lived ! In history
We read, how empires reach a glorious height,

And afterwards decline ; but otherwise
It was with him ; he never rose to fame
But afterwards, or rather previously,
Declined ; he never rose to glory, but
Skipped, as 't were, from where he should have risen,
To where he fell ; he lived before he died,
Yet died before he lived, and went to seed.
Too late to save the final lung, he left
For Borneo ; and yet this stream of which
He was so special fond, to me doth seem,
Of him to me this present hour to chat,
To me, of him especial fond, to chat,
For, " O thou creek," he said, " O running creek,"
Said Wilkins in his rhyme, " whence flow'st thou?
    where ?
Why flow'st thou ? whither ? " and the creek—why
    should   .
A running creek do otherwise ?—replies :

I flow from places up above,
    I spring from out a valley ;
And then run down you know, my love,
    Run down continu-ally.

By twenty hills I hurry down,
    And over twenty ripples;
By sixty trees, a smallish town
    Of say a hundred peoples,

Till, finally, it happens so,
    I reach the farm of Dolly;
For men go up and downward go,
    But I go downward alway.

Poor Wilkins on his way to Borneo,
At Botany-Bay, he died. Observe the bridge,
Weaklier than 't was; the -mill-dam there;
Here Dolly's farm, referred to in the verse.

I chuckle over stones and sticks,
    I laugh and gossip often;
I whistle into bays and creeks,
    I hurry down a-coughing.

Round many capes, of many shapes,
    By hook and crook I travel;

And under stones my current creeps,
And over sand and gravel.

I keep it up, while running down
Towards the farm of Dolly;
For men go up and men go down,
But I go downward alway.

But Dolly chattered more than babbling creeks;
Old Dolly; wheresoe'er you went she was;
And where she went, her tongue went always too,
As tiresome as a spinster katy-did.

My current wriggles very fast,
With bubbles floating in it;
And now a spider swimmeth past,
Or stops to breathe a minute;

And now comes sailing down a stick,
And now, perhaps, a clover;
And then the clover hits the stick,
And both go rolling over;

And yet I never stop, you know,
But hasten down to Dolly,
For men go up and downward go,
But I go downward alway.

O Daisy Peters, niece of Dolly, though !
A female of this age, yet not insane ; .
A native of our clime, and yet as good
As foreign born ; straight as a pine tree—as
A willow slim ; with violet eyes and hair
A bright and cheerful sort of reddish brown,
The hue of birch bark on the under side.

Dear Daisy ! well, I helped her much one time,
Her and the youth whom she had promised to
Be his tho' not to change her name, because
The man was Tobee Peters. cousin he
Upon her father's side ; and so her name
Continued Peters, still, you understand.
'T was thirty years ago, or nigh to that,
And pretty hard upon the mournful time,
When I and Wilkins separated here ;
I came across the bridge—'t was shaky then,

As now much more, curving across the face
Of Nature, like an ancient Roman nose—
I came across it, whistling " Scots wha' ha'e,"
And whittling on a shingle, nothing much,
'T was quite a habit then I had, and kicked
At Dolly's stable gate. 'T was out of fix
Some way, and Dolly, hearing how it squeaked,
Shrieked out, " You Daisy, run ! " but that she could
N't do : her weight was close to twenty stone :
And so she waddled out towards the barn,
And met me there, quite flustered, I observed,
And moist about the eyes ; a little *downy*,
So to speak, and red as bashful peach.

What was it? something, sure, was in the wind
Because she was n't downy, in the sense
I mean, at usual times, nor often let
A little sorrow, from her heart's deep well,
Draw up the bucket of unpleasant tears.

She told me what. They 'd fallen out, herself
And Tobee. " What about? How came it so ! "
" Oh ! nothing much," she said ; " Tobee was sort

Of—well, she knew not what, and she had said
Something, she knew not how, or why, or when,
Which, some way, made the—well, had kind of placed
Them thus." "Who did it first?" She rather thought
'T was him—or her—or neither first, perhaps,
Things somehow seemed to!" Here her tears burst
      forth,   .
And swept her choking, struggling words afar
Beyond the harbor of my open ear.

"Why do n't he come?" says I. "He will," says she.
"That 's what he wants," says she. "Well,
      what," says I,
"Prevents?" "Her aunt kept talking so," she said,
"He could n't get to say beyond a word,
But she would cut him short, and so he left,
Disgusted with her aunt and also her."

"Well, what can I do, then?" says I. "Will you?"
Says she. "Do what?" says I. "Converse with aunt
For half an hour or so, till me and Wilk
Make up?" She looked so soft, I says, "Oh yes!"

And ere I'd finished saying Yes, he came
Across the lot, a-bobbing thro' the corn.

So in I went and entered into talk
With Dolly, who was darning stockings there;
Oh! how she rattled though, and made me go
And see her Christmas pig, and told me how
He grew a pound a day, until she feared
A rush of blood to head might take him off
Ere Christmas came; and then her Shanghai fowls;
And measured one great rooster's legs four times,
To prove 't was eighteen inches long, which 't was,
Pulling a feather from his tail besides,
For me to carry to my youngest child:
She showed me next, her cow; and then began
And told me how old Farmer Huff had tried
To buy a cow, the dam of this, one time,
But she knew Farmer Huff, and would n't sell
For twice the sum; he called her crazy too,
But she·knew what it ought to bring, and he
Came after, twice, to offer more, in vain,
For she knew what a cow like that would bring,
And would n't be imposed by Huff at all;

And so she stuck; until one day, 't was March,
She said—let see—yes, sixth of March he came,
A Friday 't was—and took the old cow home
At her own price; just as she 'd said he would,
For she knew him, and what a cow like that
Had ought to bring; it was n't such a cow
As grew on every bush, she knew of that.

And when I thought she 'd done, she off again,
And told me how this present cow gave more
Than two pints more than her—and how she thought
'T would be as much as nigh a quart in June—
Until I felt as if she 'd drive me mad,
And said I must go home; and so we turned
And entered back, as Wilk and Daisy came
In front, their little matters all arranged,
As full of smiles as Dolly's cow of milk,
Talking and laughing like the babbling creek.

●

    I sweep around the mossy rocks,
      I slip beneath the rushes,
    I whisper to the hollyhocks
      That doze among the bushes.

I hop, I glide, I pop, I slide,
From unexpected places,
I make the bullfrogs blush and hide
To see their homely faces.

Through March and April, May, July,
June, August and ·September,
October and November, I
Run on, until December;

From that till first of March again,
It 's often on I 'm flowing,
And off and on I stop, and then
It 's off and on I 'm going.

And so, you know, I run and flow
With many a whirl and eddy,
While men go up and down they go,
I go down always steady.

Yes! that is true; men have their ups and downs,
And likewise I; my friends have disappeared.

In Botany-Bay doth Wilkins sleep, beside
The rushing waves of Swallawaggle's stream :
His grave th' "obscure initials W. M."
Doth bear; I saw; Dolly's swift tongue is tied
By hand of Death; and Daisy's tracks are found
Around the base of Popocatapetl,
Far from this isle; yes, ne'er a one is left.

  So Jabez Tomkin, sitting on a log,
With one foot either side, did ruminate—
Strange memories and stranger rhymes, meanwhile,
Swift passing through his head deprived of hair,
When something like a puffing made him look ;
And as he turned he saw a rosy lass
Climbing the fence; greatly to his surprise ;
And she did blush exceeding much. Her eyes
Were violet, and her hair a reddish brown,
The hue of birch-bark on the under side ;
And Jabez, more and more surprised, inquired,
"Are you from yonder farm? "—"I be," says she.
"Excuse me : stop, I beg ; and what 's your name?"
"Daisy."—"Daisy !—that 's singular," says he.
"What 's t' other?"—"Peters."—"No ! "—"Oh, yes, it
    be ! "—

"Do n't say!"—and then he looked so very queer,
That Daisy giggled, and directly he
Did also giggle, as 't were in his sleep.
"You 're much too fat, and red, and healthy-like,
To be the ghost of Daisy Peters, here-
Abouts, nigh on to thirty years ago!"
"Why, do n't you know?" says Daisy, "lor, how
    queer!
We 've come and took the farm again, you see,
Am I so like as that?—just what he said,
The stage man, coming down! In case you know
My ma, you 'd best go 'long, sir, now, with me.
Dick, he 's gone down the lane to fetch the cow;
But ma—she 's home, I know—Walk in, Walk in!"

I.

Have I been asleep, do you s'pose,
  Right here, I can't tell how?
Was I in a sort of a doze,
  While lying here . just now?

Boys were laughing together,
  Laughing and talking of me;
"Well, I guess if it 's him, it 's him,
  And if not, why who can it be?

Is it a shadow of something
  Seen with a ghastly smile,
Savages grinning together
  Upon a Cannibal isle?

93

Queer, that I hear two boys,
    Somewhere, talking of me,
" Well, I guess if it 's him, it 's him,
    And if not, why who can it be ! "

II.

Go not, Sara-jane,
    From this place and me,
Go not, Sara-jane,
    Not till after tea.
'T is n't dark, you know,
    'T is n't dark till eight,
'T is n't dark until
    Seven, at any rate.
If the happy Yes,
    You will only say,
I 'll tell Antso-phia
    You 're going to stay ;
Going to stay an hour,
    Going to stay till dusk,

Stay and drink some tea,
　Stay and eat some rusk.
I 'll tell Antso-phia,
　Tell her quick as look,
And then, Antso-phia,
　She will tell the cook;
Tell the cook the fact,
　Tell her how 't will be,
Tell her bake the rusk,
　Tell her make the tea.
Go not, Sara-jane,
　Oh, no, Sara, wait,
Stay, oh Jane, till seven,
　Sara-jane, till eight.

III.

Come out in the garden, Jane,
　For the black bear, night, has run,
Come out in the garden, Jane,
　It 's time the party was done;

And the chickens commence to cackle again,
And the cocks crow one by one.

For a breeze begins to blow,
And the planet of Jupiter, he,
Grows shaky and pale as the dawn, you know,
Comes striding over the sea,
Grows pale as the dawn keeps coming, you know,
Grows paler and paler to be.

All night have the tulips shaked
At the noise of the fiddle and drum;
All night has the trumpet-vine quivered and
quaked,
As the sounds of the dancing come;
Till chickens and cocks in the hen-roost waked,
And they stopt the fiddle and drum.

I said to the tulip, "It 's I," says I,
"Whom she likes best of them all;
When will they let her alone," says I,
"She 's tired, I know, of the ball.

Now part of the folks have said Good-bye,
  And part are there in the hall,
They 'll all be off, directly," says I,
  "And then I 'm over the wall."

I said to the pink, " Nigh over, I think,
  The dancing and glancing and fun :
O young Lloyd Lever, your hopes will sink,
  When you find the charmer is won ;
We 're one, we 're one," I remarked to the pink,
  "In spirit, already, one."

And the red of the pink went into my face,
  As I thought of your sweet, "I will ;"
And long I stood in that slippery place,
  For I heard our waterfall spill,
Spill over the rocks and run on in the race,
  The mill-race down by the mill ;
From the tree where I feebly stated my case,
  To the fence where you answered, "I will."

The drowsy buttercup went to bed,
  Nor left a lock of her hair ;

The great sunflower, he nodded his head,
  And· the poppy snored in his chair;
But the pink was n't sleepy at all, she said,
  Wishing my pleasure to share,
No tulip nor pink of them cared for bed,
  They knew I expected you there.

Queen pink of the feminine pinks, in there,
  Come out in the garden to me,
In the velvet basque . silk-lined you wear,
  Queen pink and tulip you be;
Bob out, little face, running over with hair,
  And let the hollyhocks see.

Is that the marigold's laugh I hear,
  Or the sound of her foot as 't fell?
She is coming, my duck, my dear;
  She is coming my bird, my belle;
The blood-pink cries, "She is near, she is near,"
  And the pale-pink sobs, "Do tell;"
The Snap-dragon says, "D' you see her, d' you
      see her?"
  And the tulip—"There by the well!"

She is coming, my joy, my pet;
  Let her trip it, soft as she chose,
My pulses would livelier get,
  Were I dying under the rose;
My blood flow rapider yet,
  Were I buried down under the rose;
Would start and trickle out ruby and wet,
  And bubble wherever she goes.